The
Nesting Quilt

Cathryn Falwell

Tilbury House Publishers
Thomaston, Maine

Grateful thanks to
Audrey Maynard and Meg Nobel.

Tilbury House Publishers
12 Starr Street, Thomaston, Maine 04861
800-582-1899 • www.tilburyhouse.com

First hardcover edition: May 2015
ISBN 978-0-88448-418-9
eBook ISBN 978-0-88448-419-6

Text and illustrations copyright © 2015 Cathryn Falwell

Library of Congress Cataloging-in-Publication Data

Falwell, Cathryn, author, illustrator.
  The nesting quilt / by Cathryn Falwell.
      pages   cm
  Summary: Maya's family is preparing for a new
baby and she wants to help, so she draws on her
interest in birds' nests to create a very special quilt.
  Includes information about quilt making and
instructions for making a small quilt.
  ISBN 978-0-88448-418-9 (hardcover)—
  ISBN 978-9884484196 (eBook)
[1. Quilting—Fiction. 2. Family life—Fiction.
 3. Birds—Nests—Fiction. 4. Babies—Fiction.]
 I. Title.
PZ7.F198Nes 2015
[E]—dc23   2014042371

Printed in China by Shenzhen Caimei Printing Co., Ltd.,
February 2015 (43097-0/101714.3)
15 16 17 18 19 20 FCL 5 4 3 2 1

For
my dear aunt,
Wanda Chauvin

Our house is SO busy.
We are getting ready
for our new baby.
I'm going to be
a big sister soon.
"We're nesting,
  Maya!"
says Nana.
"Just like the birds,"
  I tell her.

Nana and I love birds,
and we love to look
for their nests, too.
Once we saw a
huge eagle nest
made from
branches and sticks.
Eagle nests
need to be strong
for big hungry eaglets.

Another time I
was really lucky.
I spotted a teeny tiny
hummingbird nest
woven with
spiderweb silk.
Hummingbird nests
can stretch when the
baby birds grow.

Some birds make nests
on the ground.
We saw a loon nest
right beside the lake.
Once the loon chicks
hatch, it's easy
for them to get into
the water and swim.

Wood ducks make
their nest in a hole
high up in a tree.
When the ducklings
are only one day old,
they jump
all the way down
and land safely
in the leaves.

So just like the birds,
we are nesting.
Everyone is helping to
get ready for our baby.
But what can I do?

Nana and I go outside.
We watch a small bird
with a tiny twig in her beak.
"That little finch
is nesting, too, Maya,"
says Nana.

Suddenly I have an idea.
I want to make
a nest for our baby.
But it can't be a nest
made of sticks and leaves
like the birds make.

Then the little finch
comes back.
She swoops down and
snaps up a scrap
of Nana's blue cloth.
"She's going to use it
in her nest!" says Nana.
Now I know.
I want to make
a soft and cozy nest
for our baby!

I make a drawing
and show it to Nana.
She says she can help.
We are going to
make a quilt nest
for our baby.
We sit on her bed
and look at books
to get ideas.

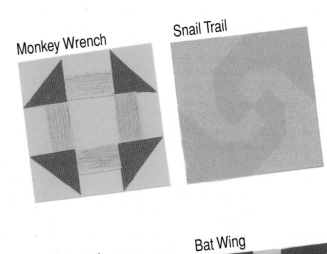

Monkey Wrench

Snail Trail

Maple Leaf

Bat Wing

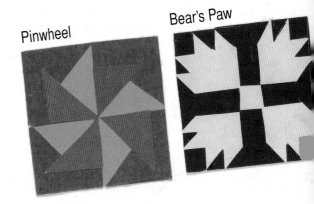

Pinwheel

Bear's Paw

We find lots of things
to make the quilt.
Nana even lets me cut my
old pajamas into squares.

Then we arrange the pieces
into a picture that looks
like my drawing.

When the design is ready,
Nana shows me how to
sew the shapes together.
Tiny stitches are hard to make,
but Nana and Mama help me.

We sew and sew,
and we
wait and wait.

Then finally,
my baby brother comes!
He's soft like feathers and
hungry like a baby bird.

We go into his room
and I unroll my gift.
"See? I made a
soft and cozy
nest for you!"

Mama lays him down
and he smiles
right up at me.

Suddenly, we hear
a lot of loud chirping.
When I look
out the window,
I see the little finch
and a nest
full of tiny birds!

Now our little baby
is sound asleep —
warm and cozy
in his own little
nest.

You will need:

❖ Scraps of cloth to make nine 6-inch squares. Different colors and patterns will make your quilt more interesting. Be sure to ask before you cut up old clothes! Sturdy cotton works best. T-shirts are too stretchy and hard to sew. You will sew these nine squares together to make the patchwork block front of the quilt.

❖ Two large squares of cloth, 16 inches by 16 inches each. One can be cotton, or something soft like flannel. This piece will be the back of your quilt.

The other large square can be fleece, a piece of terrycloth toweling, or cotton quilt batting. This will be the middle of the of the quilt.

❖ Scissors, a ruler, a right triangle, a pencil, cardboard, straight pins, a needle, and sewing thread.

❖ To tie the quilt together, you will also need about 24 inches of embroidery thread or thin yarn and a larger needle.

Make a Quilt!

Here's how you can sew a little quilt for a special small friend.

Use a ruler and a triangle to draw a six-inch square on a piece of light cardboard. You can use an empty cereal box. Carefully cut out the square on the lines.

Now trace the square onto your cloth, using a pencil or ballpoint pen. Carefully cut it out. Make nine cloth squares.

On the back of each square, draw a line 1/2 inch inside each edge, to guide your sewing.

Pin two squares together, with the "nice" sides facing each other. Using small stitches, sew along one edge on the line you drew.

Sew one more square onto these two to make a row of three squares. Take out the pins.

Ask an adult to help you iron the squares open and flat. Make two more rows.

Next, match up the squares and pin two rows together, nice sides facing again, and sew a straight line that connects the two rows. Add the third row the same way.

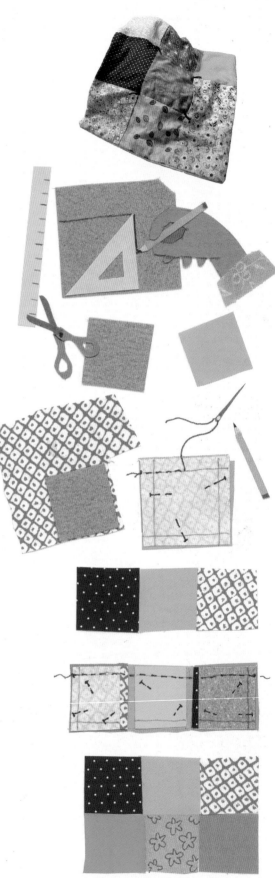

Now you will have a block that looks like a tic-tac-toe board, with nine squares.

Ask an adult to help iron it flat. It should be about 16 inches by 16 inches.

Now you can make a big sandwich with all the pieces! Put your patchwork front of the quilt down on the table, nice side up.

Put the back piece on next—nice side down. Carefully match the corners.

Last, put the soft middle piece on top. This piece will turn into the filling! Pin the sandwich all the way around.

Next you are going to sew around the whole thing, but leave an opening on one edge about 5 inches long.

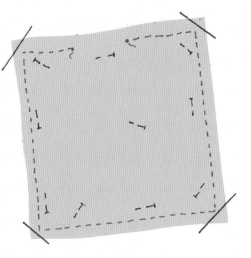

The sandwich is going to be a little hard to sew by hand if the fabrics are heavy, so if you know someone with a sewing machine, ask them to help you do this part.

When the edges are sewn together, carefully cut off the corners. Be sure not to cut too close to the stitching.

Turn the page for more. . .

Turn the page for more. . .

There are many ways to sew squares together to make quilts. You can practice your design with squares of colored paper.

Now turn the whole thing inside out through the opening, making sure that the middle piece becomes the filling. Fold in the edges of the opening and stitch it closed. Iron the quilt flat, then pin it together.

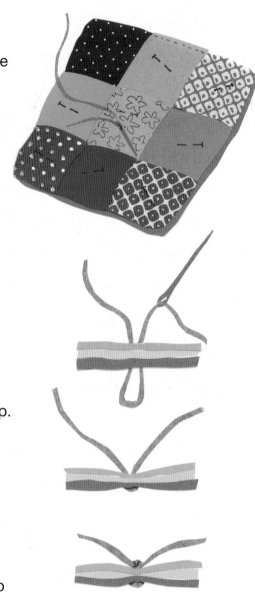

The last step will help keep your quilt together. You will make four small ties using yarn or embroidery thread. The ties will be in the corners of the middle square.

To make each tie, poke the needle carefully through all three layers from the top. Leave a "tail" of yarn on the top.

Then turn the quilt over, and poke the needle back through just a little way from where it came out.

Tie the two ends tightly together. Leave about an inch of yarn on each tail and cut. Do this on the other three corners, too. Remove the pins.

You have made a beautiful quilt for a special small friend!

People all over the world make quilts to keep their families warm and to give as gifts for special occasions.

The kind of quilt Maya makes is called a ***patchwork*** or ***scrap quilt.*** She sewed together scraps of Nana's cloth to make a nest design.

Quilts are often made using patterns that were invented long ago. Scraps are cut into shapes and sewn together into blocks. Lots of blocks are put together to make the quilt.

Turn back to the page where Maya and Nana are looking at quilt books and you will see some of the blocks and their funny names!

For more quilting fun, including instructions for making Maya's nest quilt, please visit:
www.cathrynfalwell.com